Nate saw the ball heading into the corner of the net. He felt his heart sink as...

But Jared dove.

He stretched all the way out, his body almost on the ground. He slammed the ball with his fist and drove it wide of the goal.

There was no way that Nate could have made the play. Not today.

Books about the kids from
Angel Park:

BACKUP GOALIE

By Dean Hughes

Illustrated by Dennis Lyall

Bullseye Books • Alfred A. Knopf
New York

Library of Congress Cataloging-in-Publication Data
Hughes, Dean, 1943–
Backup goalie / by Dean Hughes ; illustrated by Dennis Lyall.
p.   cm. — (Angel Park soccer stars ; 5)
Summary: When Nate Matheson, Angel Park's regular goalie, gets
injured, he has to train Jared Trajillo to replace him.
ISBN 0-679-82638-6 (pbk.) — ISBN 0-679-92638-0 (lib. bdg.)
[1. Soccer—Fiction.] I. Lyall, Dennis, ill. II. Title.
III. Series: Hughes, Dean, 1943– Angel Park soccer stars ; 5.
PZ7.H87312Bac 1992 [Fic]—dc20 91-4714
RL: 4.5
First Bullseye Books edition: May 1992

Manufactured in the United States of America
10 9 8 7 6 5 4 3 2 1

for Russell Boyd

★ 1 ★

Flying High

=====

Nate Matheson was having fun. His team, the Angel Park Pride, was playing great.

And so was he.

He was playing like a world-class goalie.

Halftime was coming up, and he still had a shutout. The Pride was ahead, 3 to 0. And the attack was really rolling, with some of the players pouring on the pressure.

Lian Jie, the rookie midfielder, had scored his first goal of the year.

Heidi Wells, the Pride's best forward, had also scored a goal, and she had been stealing the ball all day.

Jacob Scott had gotten the other goal. He had jumped high and slammed home a header—something he had not been able to do early in the season when he had first started playing forward.

Clayton Lindsay, the other midfielder, was playing great as usual. He was controlling the ball in the middle, and he had made the passes that had led to all three goals.

All that would have been good any day, but this was against the San Lorenzo Kickers!

San Lorenzo had one of the best teams in the league. They were in first place, one game ahead of the Pride. Angel Park had beaten them once before, but it had been a tough battle that time.

Nate told himself not to get overconfident. He had to concentrate.

Still, he knew the players believed in themselves now. They were playing hard—and smart—and their training was paying off.

But now was no time to get cocky. He adjusted his headband and hunched over, ready for whatever the Kickers had for him.

Peter Vandegraff, the boy from Holland

who was such a great forward, was dribbling toward the goal area, angling in from the left. Nate moved to the left side of the goal.

Sterling Malone, the Pride's fastest defender, was keeping himself between Peter and the goal. He faked a tackle, but he didn't take any chances. Peter had some great moves.

Peter stopped driving, dropped back a little, and then passed off to his brother, Klaus, the other forward.

Klaus took the ball across the field in front of the goal area. Tammy Hill, a hard-nosed fullback, marked him close, and then Brian Rohatinsky, the sweeper, doubled him.

Nate smiled as he watched the defense shift and cover. It was a beautiful thing to see.

Patty Pinelli, the Kickers' feisty left wing, tried to break past Adam Snarr for a pass. She was open for a moment, but Tammy guarded Klaus so well that he couldn't kick the ball to Patty.

As Klaus looked for someone to pass to,

Tammy stepped in and knocked the ball against his shins. The ball bounced away— but the Kickers got a break.

Peter darted to the ball and slammed a quick pass right to Patty. Adam had let Patty slip away, and she was wide open. She rushed at the goal, drew in Tammy to guard her, and then shot a perfect pass to Klaus.

Klaus took the ball out of the air with his left foot, made a quick move to his right, and then blasted a shot at the net.

Nate was in a good position, but the ball was coming like a bullet. He reacted just in time to get a hand out and flick the ball off to the side.

It was a fantastic save, but the ball was still alive, and Patty got to it. She pounded a shot right back at the goal.

This time Nate had to jump high and to his left. He caught the ball with his finger-tips and pulled it in.

"Great save!" Tammy shouted, but Nate was too busy to think about it. He jumped up and made a quick throw to Lian.

"Attack!" Nate shouted, and the Pride

blasted away. The Kickers reversed and tried to get back, but the Pride had the jump on them.

Clayton took a pass from Lian. He charged all out, kicking the ball ahead of him. But as soon as a fullback moved in, Clayton flicked the ball back to Lian.

Lian was small but quick. He darted to the right and passed off to Chris Baca, the right wing. Chris passed ahead to Heidi, and she made a break straight to the goal.

Clayton was racing down the middle of the field. A fullback was trying to stay with him.

Clayton cut toward the corner of the goal just as Heidi spotted him and lobbed a pass.

But the pass was ahead of him.

Clayton was running hard to catch up. At the same time, the goalie charged after the ball.

From the other end of the field, Nate thought the pass would be too long. But then he saw Clayton jump.

Not jump, but dive!

He stretched himself out and hit the ball

with his forehead, just before the ball was going to hit the ground.

The goalie got there an instant too late. He dove, too, and reached for the ball.

But Clayton *banged* the ball past him and into the net.

It was an amazing shot.

And a big goal.

The Pride had the Kickers 4 to 0 now, and it seemed that nothing could go wrong.

Nate ran all the way to the centerline and yelled, "That was a *miracle* shot, Clayton. Way to go!"

Clayton was dancing up and down in the middle of all the Pride players. "Miracle *shot?*" he yelled back. "What about those two saves? You're the one shutting out these guys!"

The Vandegraff brothers were walking slowly up the field. They were both great players, and they weren't used to losing.

Nate saw them talking to each other. He could guess what they were saying.

But Nate thought, "Let 'em try to make a comeback. We're not lucking out today.

We're *playing*." He also knew that he had never played better.

The Vandegraffs did try to get something going as time in the first half was running out.

Peter worked the ball in and got off a solid shot. But Nate made another amazing save. He sensed where the ball was heading, dove, and caught the ball just off the grass. Then he jumped up and cleared the ball well up the field.

A few seconds later the halftime whistle blew.

As Nate trotted to the side of the field, he liked what he saw. All the Pride players were running, and they looked as fresh as if they had only played for a few minutes.

But the Kickers were walking. And most of them had their heads down. They looked beaten.

Coach Toscano called the players together. He was even more excited than usual. "This is what soccer is all about," he told them. "You're playing the game the way it's supposed to be played. We made some mistakes on defense, but thanks to Nate we didn't have to pay for them. He made some *amazing* saves."

Heidi looked over at Nate and grinned. She whispered, "I knew that someday you would catch on to this game."

Jacob was lying on his back next to Nate. He laughed at Heidi, and then he used his announcer's voice. "Soccer fans," he said, "it's a great day in the history of sports. Mild-mannered goalie Nate Matheson is playing up to the level of Heidi Wells. This may never have happened before."

Then Jacob changed his voice and pretended to be a second announcer. "That's right, Frank. But he'll never play as well as Jacob Scott. Did you see the header he made today? What a player that boy is!"

Nate laughed, and then he leaned back on the grass. He let the autumn sun bake into his face. He felt great.

Nate wished that his parents had come to the match—which would have made things even better. But Nate's dad *was* showing more interest in the game all the time—and that was some real progress.

The coach made some changes in the

lineup before the second half started. And before the players ran back onto the field, he told them, "Okay, now, let's stay after them. Don't let down just because you're ahead."

So the Pride players charged back out to the field. Nate trotted to the goal area and got himself ready. He hoped his teammates would remember what the coach had just told them.

Soon after the second half started, Klaus Vandegraff brought the ball into Pride territory again. He looked determined. The Kickers' coach had really chewed on his players. Klaus was out to turn things around—quickly. Nate could see that.

Klaus ran hard, with Sterling right at his shoulder. But then he made a quick stop and shook Sterling loose for a moment. He tried to loop a pass to his brother.

But Sterling shot out a foot and blocked the pass.

The ball looped in the air and Heidi charged in, trapped it, and then blasted ahead. The Pride team jumped out ahead of the Kickers and raced up the field.

Jacob ran with Heidi, and the two seemed on their way to taking the ball to the goal.

But Heidi tried to pass off, and she led Jacob a little too much. A fullback was able to break in and stop the pass.

The Kickers came back hard. This time when Klaus got the ball, he didn't dribble as far. He kicked a long lead pass to Patty Pinelli. She dribbled a few steps toward the goal and then saw Peter working his way into the goal area.

Patty centered a pass, and Peter timed it perfectly. He got up in the air, ready to head the ball in.

But Sterling jumped with him, and so did Nate. Nate reached high, snagged the ball, and then pulled it in to his chest.

He already knew that he wanted to get the ball out quickly and . . .

But as he landed, pain shot through his ankle.

He crumpled to the ground.

He had landed on the outside of his foot and had twisted his ankle—badly.

Nate didn't want to be a baby. He tried not to scream, but he rolled around on the ground and moaned. He had never done anything that hurt this much.

But even with all the pain, he was already thinking, "No, not now. Not when we are doing so well."

★ 2 ★

Crash Landing

Nate's pain let up a little after a while. But only a little. He knew he couldn't play.

The coach got Sterling to help him, and they carried Nate off the field. Then he had Chris, who wasn't playing right now, run and call Nate's father at his office.

Nate hoped his dad would be slow getting there. Even though he was still hurting, he wanted to see the rest of the game.

Nate hoped the players could keep playing well and hang on to the win. But he knew—and so did everyone else—that the Pride didn't have another strong goalie.

And that could be a problem—big time.

"Jared," the coach called. "Get a goalie shirt on. I want you to go in for Nate."

Nate and Coach Toscano had been working with Jared during practice. Jared had the size and ability to be a good goalie.

He just didn't have much experience.

Now he would get some—fast.

As Jared ran out on the field, Nate finally had time to think. His ankle was throbbing with pain, and it was already starting to swell. What if his ankle was broken? He could be finished for the whole season, just when the team was coming together.

With a win over the Kickers today, they could move into a tie for first.

But if the Pride blew this lead now, they would be two games back into third place. They could never catch the Kickers if that happened.

Jared was jumping around in the goal area, trying to warm himself up. He looked nervous.

The Kickers were good sports. Some of the players had already told Nate that they hoped he was okay. But they had to be a little bit relieved with Nate out of the game.

When the match got going again, Nate could see that the Kickers were feeling more confident.

They were breaking more quickly than before, and they were all staying active, making the defense work.

Peter made a good pass to the wing, who ran up the touchline and then dropped the ball back to a midfielder. The midfielder quickly sent a looping pass toward the goal.

Sterling and Tammy kept Klaus from getting off a shot. But the ball hit Sterling and bounced in front of the goal area.

Peter raced in and controlled the ball. Then he fired a long shot. Nate held his breath, but Jared moved into a good position.

He caught the ball and . . .

But he didn't catch it!

He was right there, but he let the ball slam

off his chest and roll in front of the goal.

Pinelli was on the ball in an instant. She trapped it and took a quick look to the left. Jared broke in that direction, but Pinelli popped the ball the other way and into the net.

Just like that!

It was 4 to 1, with lots and lots of time left to play.

The Pride players yelled back and forth to each other not to let up on attack—not to get too careful. They came hard, and a couple of times they almost scored. But the Kickers were playing tough now. They were really working on defense.

Nate lay back on the grass and shut his eyes. He was hurting. But more than that, he could hardly stand to watch. He wanted time to pass—with no more scores for San Lorenzo.

Still, he didn't want his father to come too soon. He wanted to be sure of the win before he left.

Coach Toscano kept checking with him.

"Maybe we should try to reach your mother," he said. "Maybe your dad is in a meeting or something. I hate to wait too long."

"I'm okay, Coach," Nate told him. "I don't think it's serious. I think I'll be able to play . . . before too long." But he didn't say, "on Thursday," the day of the next match. He really doubted he could do that.

And then his worries got worse.

Angel Park was doing well. Billy Bacon was in the game now as a fullback, and he was fresh and strong. He was staying right on Klaus. But Klaus had better speed.

Klaus slipped ahead of Billy, and a midfielder shot him a low lead pass.

The defense was in a good position, however, and Klaus really didn't have much of a shot. But he powered the ball toward the goal anyway, hoping for a rebound—or a mistake.

And a mistake was what he got.

Jared had time, but instead of getting in front of the ball, he tried to reach for it. The ball popped right through his hands.

And it rolled into the net.

And now what Nate had feared most was happening.

The match would be a battle from this point. A lot of time was still left, and the Kickers were within two goals.

Nate lay back again. Maybe it would be best to head to the hospital now. If a disaster was about to happen, at least he wouldn't have to watch it.

But things started to get better. The Pride players worked hard. They played frantic defense. They held the Kickers away from the goal area.

And they put a lot of pressure on the Kickers' goalie.

The Pride didn't score, but they were close a few times. Nate was starting to think that his teammates were going to get that fifth goal and push the Kickers back out of the match.

But it just didn't happen. And then Nate saw his dad's car pull into the parking lot.

When Mr. Matheson got to Nate, he bent down and said, "How bad is it?"

"Not too bad. I should be able to—" But his dad reached for the ankle and Nate suddenly said, "Don't touch it!"

"Sounds pretty bad if it hurts just to touch it."

Nate knew that was true, but he didn't like to admit it. And yet he was glad that his dad was so concerned.

Dad was wearing his dark business suit, and he looked out of place compared to most of the other parents, who were wearing jeans or shorts. "I'm sorry you had to come over," Nate told him. "Were you in a meeting or something?"

"Yes, I was. But that doesn't matter. I had been planning to get away just for the end of the game."

"I'd still like to stay till the end, Dad. We're up four to two on the Kickers. If we can hang on—"

Nate heard a roar from the other side of the field.

He looked around, and he saw all the Kickers jumping up and down in the goal area. A lot of them were slapping Klaus on the back.

Jared was standing with his hands on his hips. He was staring straight at the grass.

It didn't take Sherlock Holmes to figure out that the score was now 4 to 3.

"All right," Coach Toscano was yelling. "Don't let it bother you, Jared. Come on, players, let's get on the attack and score one."

"How much time is left?" Nate yelled to Henry White.

"Under four minutes."

The coach was sending Henry in the game now, along with Chris and Tammy.

"You gotta do it!" Nate yelled to them. "Pack in on defense and help Jared out."

"Don't worry," Tammy yelled to him. "We won't let you down. We're not going to lose this one."

And somehow Nate believed that. "Dad, it's only four minutes. Let's stay."

"We ought to get you to the emergency room before that ankle swells too much."

"I know. But it's only four minutes."

His dad nodded. "But lie back and rest."

Nate tried, but he couldn't do it. He was soon sitting up again.

The Pride players were playing hard-nosed defense. They were going all out. Klaus and Peter were using all the moves they had. But the Angel Park defenders were right on them.

And then Heidi made a move behind Klaus and stripped the ball.

The Kickers had pulled their fullbacks all the way into the attack, and no one was back near the goal. Heidi shot upfield ahead of everyone.

A defender chased after her.

Jacob also raced up the field and caught up. Heidi hit him with a good pass. At the same time, Nate saw Clayton running in from the left.

The Pride had the Kickers' defender three-on-one, and the only thing they had to be careful about now was an offside call. And that meant staying behind the defender when they didn't have the ball.

But they worked their passes just right. They kept the defender guessing and turning. They didn't run ahead of him.

When Clayton ended up with the ball close to the goal area, he pushed straight ahead. Then, just as he seemed ready to shoot, he dropped the ball back to Heidi.

The goalie had taken on Clayton, and now he was all the way to the left side of the goal.

Heidi had a wide open shot, and she punched the ball into the goal.

Nate finally let his breath flow again. He shot his hands in the air and cheered. But the motion jerked his body, and his ankle suddenly came alive with pain.

Nate had had enough. "Okay, Dad," he said. "We've got 'em. Let's go." Now that he felt sure this match was in the bag, his biggest concern was being able to play again— as soon as possible.

And so while the Pride celebrated their goal, Mr. Matheson picked up Nate and carried him toward the car.

Some of the players ran over and wished Nate well.

Nate was already thinking about the next match. The Bandits were not as good as the Kickers. But if Jared had to play goalie . . . No. That was not good to think about.

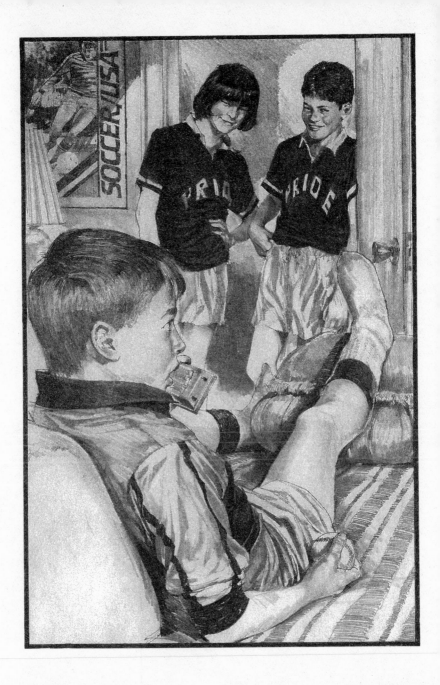

★ 3 ★

Out of Action

The news at the hospital was good . . . and bad.

Nate's ankle was not broken, but it was badly sprained. The doctor wrapped it with a cold pack.

"How soon do you think I can play soccer?" Nate asked him.

"Well, it's a little hard to say," the doctor told him. "But I doubt you'll be able to play for two weeks. And even then it will have to be wrapped very carefully. For a week I want you to keep your weight off it. You'll have to use crutches."

Nate felt sick. Today was Monday. The next *big* match was only a week from Thursday. His dream of having a great season was slipping away.

Coach Toscano had gotten to the hospital. He was standing by the doctor. "Don't worry, Nate," he said. "I'm just glad it isn't broken."

Nate couldn't believe that the coach wasn't more upset. "Will Jared play goalie?" he asked.

"Sure. We'll work with him. You can help him a lot. He'll do better than he did today."

Nate wondered.

A nurse wheeled Nate outside, and his dad helped him get into the car. By that time Nate was almost in tears.

When his dad walked around the car and got in on his side, he said, "Well, Nate, it could have been a lot worse. At least you won't miss the whole season."

"By the time I get back, it won't matter," Nate said. He looked out the window, away from his dad.

"What do you mean?" his dad asked as he backed the car out of the parking place.

"Jared will have to play goalie. And he *stinks*. He'll probably lose every game for us while I'm gone."

Nate knew that was a rotten thing to say about one of his teammates, but he was *feel-*

ing rotten. It was better to be angry than to let himself cry.

"Is he really *that* bad?"

"Yes. I could have stopped all those shots that he let get by him."

"Can't you work with him?"

"Sure. But it takes time. And besides, I don't think he'll ever be very good."

Dad didn't say anything for a while. Nate kept looking out the window, but he wasn't really seeing anything. All he knew was that everything was ruined.

"Nate," Dad finally said, "I know you want to win the championship. But there's a lot more to soccer—or any sport—than just winning."

Nate didn't want to hear a speech from his dad right now. His dad didn't really care that much about soccer anyway.

"It's when things go bad that a team finds out what it's made of. The same for a person."

"Dad, for once I wanted to be on a team that *won*."

"Well, then, do what it takes to make it happen. You've got three days to teach Jared everything you can."

Nate thought about that. The game on

Thursday was against the Bandits, who weren't all that good. Maybe somehow Jared could get through that one.

After that, the Pride had a bye. So Nate would have until the next Thursday to get back on his feet. That wasn't two weeks, but it *was* ten days, and maybe Nate's ankle would get better faster than the doctor thought.

If Jared could get the team through one game, maybe Angel Park still had a chance.

"You know, Nate," Dad said, "being a team player means that you're willing to—"

"I know all that stuff, Dad."

"I'm not sure you do." Dad waited for Nate to look his way. Then he said, "You need to show that you not only care about winning but that you care about Jared. Just think how he's feeling right now."

Nate really hadn't thought about that. He knew Jared had to be relieved that the Pride hadn't lost. But they had barely hung on. The guy was probably already scared to death about the next match.

Thinking about it that way, the whole picture looked sort of different.

When Nate and his dad got home, Dad

helped him to his bedroom. Nate said he had to make some calls, so Dad brought him the cordless phone.

Nate called Heidi first, and then Jacob. Neither one was home. He found out why when they showed up at his house. But by then Nate was making another call.

He was calling Jared.

The first thing Jared asked was, "How long before you can play again?"

"I don't know," Nate said. "I'll miss the game with the Bandits, but maybe I can be back for the Tornadoes next week."

Jared was quiet for a moment, and then he said, "If we lose to the Bandits, our season is down the drain anyway."

"We can beat 'em, Jared," Nate told him.

"Not with me as goalie. I can't stop anything."

Nate looked up and saw Heidi and Jacob standing in his doorway. He motioned for them to come in, and then he said, "Jared, don't talk that way. Tomorrow after school let's get together and practice. We'll get some other players to take shots, and I'll show you some more stuff."

Jared didn't answer.

"Is that okay?"

"I don't know. I don't really want to do it. Why doesn't the coach let Billy take over? He's played goalie before."

"I know. But he's short, and he's not very quick. You'll be better than he is—once you learn a few things."

Again there was a long pause, and then Jared said, "Nate, I know I'm going to lose the game."

"No, you won't, Jared. We have three days. We'll get you ready. Okay?"

Finally Jared said, "Okay," but he didn't sound very convinced.

When Nate set the phone down, Heidi walked over to him.

"Don't try to be brave," Heidi said. "We *know*. We talked to the doctor and found out you only have six months to live."

"Only if you drive me nuts."

"Hey, it's great you can laugh. That's the attitude we want to see. But don't worry. We're going to be by your side. We're going to make these last months as happy as possible."

"Yeah, well, thanks a lot."

"And after you're gone, we'll take care of your soccer ball. We'll juggle it every day, take it for walks—kiss it good night."

"If you want," Jacob said, "I could move in here and replace you. Your parents might miss you—a little—but I could help them forget. And I wouldn't mind. I don't have a TV in *my* room."

"Hey, can I have all your stuff?" Heidi asked. "Jacob can have the TV, but I've really been wanting a mountain bike."

"Have I ever told you two what jerks you are?" Nate said. He was smiling now, and he did feel a little better.

"Yeah, I think you've mentioned it a time or two," Heidi said. She sat down on the bed and patted Nate on the head. His white-blond hair was still matted on his forehead where his headband had held it during the match. "But the thing is, we know you're not in your right mind after your injury. We don't pay any attention to your wild ravings."

"The doctor said I'm out for maybe two weeks. But I'm going to try to be back for the game a week from Thursday."

Heidi nodded. "Do you think Jared can do it?"

"I don't know. But we can try to get him ready."

"He doesn't have very good hands," Jacob said. "That one shot slipped right through his fingers."

"I know," Nate said. "But if he had been in front of the ball, he would have been okay. He just has to learn to position himself better."

"He doesn't have your reactions," Heidi said.

Nate knew that was probably true. But he didn't want to say it. And besides, he was thinking sort of differently about it now. "Jared feels rotten," he said. "We need to help him."

"What does he feel rotten about?" Heidi asked.

"About the match today. But mostly he thinks we'll lose the game on Thursday, and it will be his fault."

"I don't blame him for being scared," Jacob said.

"I don't either. But if we can help him,

and we can win that one game, he'd feel great."

"Well, then, let's do it," Heidi said. She patted Nate on the head again. "Oh, Nate, you're so wonderful. Only six months to live and you're thinking of everyone but yourself."

"That's just the kind of guy I am," Nate said. "I can't help it."

"This is like the ending to a really stupid movie," Jacob said.

"And Nate's the *star*," Heidi added.

Nate lifted his eyes to the ceiling and sighed, and then he mumbled, "What a beautiful scene this is, too. If only you two were as brave and kind as I am. Instead of a couple of jerks."

"Grab his foot and twist it," Heidi said. "I'll hold him."

Even the thought of it hurt Nate.

Still, once the "jerks" were gone, he told himself that somehow he was going to get back on his feet for that game with the Tornadoes. He just *had* to.

★ 4 ★

From the Sidelines

The next afternoon Nate met his friends at the soccer field. His dad had to drive him over, and then Nate hiked across the park on his new crutches.

He stood behind the goal while Jared tried to stop the shots that Heidi and Jacob blasted at him.

"Get your whole body in front of the ball whenever you can," he told Jared, and he had him practice doing that.

Nate also worked on Jared's positioning in the goal. He told him how to cut off the shooter's angle by coming out of the goal.

As Jared tried to stop shots, Nate called out instructions. "Spread your hands more.

And once you catch the ball, pull it in against your chest."

Jared listened and tried to do the things Nate talked about. But he didn't show a lot of confidence in himself. Once when he let a ball go through his hands and between his legs, he got mad at himself and kicked at the goalpost.

"Jared," Nate told him, "that could happen to anyone. It was a hard shot. But it won't get through your legs if you keep your feet a little closer together."

Nate had Heidi and Jacob hit some low rolling shots, and he had Jared practice moving behind the ball and getting his legs in the right position.

Jared caught on quickly.

Nate was soon feeling a lot better. Jared was a good athlete—better than Nate had thought. He was tall, and he was a good jumper. He just didn't have much experience in the position. And now that he knew he had to learn a lot—and learn it fast—he was really working.

What Jared lacked were Nate's quick reactions. And that couldn't be taught. But after an hour or so of practice, the easy shots were not getting by him.

Nate knew Jared was going to give up some goals, but if the defense could keep down the number of good shots, maybe Jared could manage all right.

Jared was looking a lot more confident by the time the kids ended their practice. Heidi told him, "Jared, if you can improve that much in one practice, you're going to be a *great* goalie. I doubt we'll even want Nate back."

"No, he's still a *lot* better than me," Jared said.

Jared was a quiet boy. He didn't joke around a lot the way Heidi did. But he was smiling a little, and his dark eyes had brightened. Nate could see that he was not as nervous about the position as he had been before.

On Wednesday the whole team practiced together, and then Jacob and Heidi stayed and worked with Jared again. Again Nate watched and gave advice, and this time so did Coach Toscano.

Jared worked until the sweat was running off him. He was starting to look really tired. But he stayed at it.

It was the coach who finally said, "Okay, Jared, that's enough for today. You're coming along great."

Jared looked down and said, "Thanks."

The coach walked over and put his arm around Jared's shoulder. "When you get in a match, it's easy to forget some of these things we've been telling you. So you can expect to mess up a time or two. That's going to happen to anyone."

"If I mess up a time or two, we might lose," Jared said. Nate thought he saw the worry come back into his eyes.

"Maybe. Maybe not. But you can't expect to be perfect. The greatest goalkeepers in the world aren't perfect."

"The big thing, Jared," Nate said, "is that you can't let a mistake upset you. If you mess up and give up a goal, just keep hanging in there. Heidi and Jacob will score some goals for you."

"That's right," Jacob said. "We promise." He grinned, with the split between his front teeth showing. "And we're going to play defense like a bunch of maniacs."

"Speak for yourself," Heidi said. "I'm a refined woman."

Jared grinned, and so did the others.

Nate thought maybe Jared could do it. Jared was starting to believe in himself, and the Paseo Bandits weren't one of the better teams in the league. They had Kyle Oshima, but they didn't have enough good players to compete for the championship.

So Nate went to the game on Thursday, still on crutches but full of hope. He stood on the sidelines near Jared's goal, and he yelled to Jared to be *tough*.

Jared held a thumb up, and he got ready. He looked fine. He made a couple of stops, and he remembered all the things Nate and Coach Toscano had been teaching him.

A few minutes into the match Oshima got off a long shot. Jared made a good stop. The ball bounced toward the goal, and Jared got in front of it, scooped it up against his chest, and protected it.

It was exactly what Nate had shown him.

But then Jared got in too much of a hurry to get the ball out to his teammates. He wasn't a very good punter yet. Nate had told him to roll the ball to Clayton or to someone who was good at taking the ball up the field.

But Jared tried to toss the ball to Clayton too quickly, and Wadley, the Bandits' big forward, saw his chance. He broke in and stole the ball.

Wadley took one step and *wham*, jammed a hard shot right past Jared and into the goal.

Nate realized that he had spent so much time with Jared working on blocks and defensive positioning that he hadn't really taught him enough about directing the ball to the attack team.

"Don't worry about it," Nate yelled to Jared. "That's happened to me before. You made a great stop. Just take your time a little in getting the ball back out."

But Jared looked sick. He had his hands on his knees, and he was staring straight at the grass, just like in the last game. Nate knew the confidence they had worked on during the last few days had suddenly sunk into the gutter.

The Pride needed to get something going so that some of the pressure would be off Jared.

But that's not what happened.

The Bandits seemed to sense their chance. They were all yelling about the weak goalie. "We can score on this guy—no problem!" one of their midfielders kept yelling. He was a kid named Reilly, who talked a lot better game then he played.

Jared was twice as good a soccer player as this kid. But Jared heard the words. He glanced over at Nate, and Nate saw the doubt.

"You're okay," Nate yelled. "That's just one goal. Remember what I told you. Hang in there and we'll get 'em."

But now the Paseo attack was coming again, and Oshima was working hard to get another shot at "that loser of a goalie."

Oshima passed to Cheri Beesley, the girl who played right wing, and then he floated back toward the middle of the field.

He trotted along and let Sterling think he wasn't doing much. And then—*zap*—he spun and cut to his right. He raced toward the goal area with Sterling a half step behind.

Beesley tried to lift a crossing pass, but Chris Baca got in her way. She couldn't get much on the ball. It bounced toward Oshima too slowly, and his chance for a quick shot was lost.

But Oshima changed angles and ran to the ball. When he picked it up, his back was to Sterling. He dribbled to his left a little and faked to his right. And then, just when it seemed he was going to go for the goal, he dropped a pass back to Beesley.

At the same moment, Oshima spun around Sterling and darted for the goal. Beesley knew exactly what Oshima was going to do, and this time she was able to get the pass up in the air.

Jared saw what was happening, and he broke toward Oshima. He got himself into the best position he could, and he jumped for the ball, but Oshima was in front of him.

Oshima drove the ball with his head, right into the net that Jared had left wide open.

2 to 0.

Nate felt sick. But he was already yelling, "Jared, that wasn't your fault. You did what you had to do."

Nate knew that if anyone was to blame it was Sterling for letting Oshima get past him. And it was Chris's fault for letting the wing get free to make the pass.

But mostly it was just a great play by the attacking team. That was going to happen sometimes.

Jared didn't seem to see it that way, however.

He wasn't throwing a temper tantrum. He wasn't kicking or stomping or yelling. He was looking at the grass again.

And Nate knew exactly what he was thinking.

The chances for a championship were going down the drain. And Jared was sure it was all his fault.

★ 5 ★

Deep Trouble

The second goal seemed to wake up the Pride. Nate saw Heidi call the players together in the middle of the field. He knew what she was telling them.

Angel Park had to get going and take some pressure off Jared. They needed to score, and they needed to get all over the Bandits on defense.

Nate could see the difference when the action started again.

The defense got very busy, and Heidi led the way. She met a midfielder and took him on. She moved in close and knocked the ball right between his feet. And then she darted around him and took control of the ball.

Lian was right there to take a pass, and he burst upfield. Heidi ran with him, and so did Clayton. A couple of fullbacks were back, but they didn't have the speed to stay with the Pride attack.

One of the fullbacks got in front of Lian and tried to block his path to the goal. When Lian made a move to get past, he stumbled. For a moment Nate thought Lian had lost the ball.

But even though he was off balance, Lian saw Jacob coming up fast. He nudged the ball out to him. About that time Clayton and Heidi were both breaking to get free from their defenders.

Jacob faked a pass to Heidi, and then he drove straight for the goal. He was guarded and had no chance for a shot, but Heidi stopped suddenly, and her defender slipped by.

Jacob slapped a pass to her, and she caught it against the inside of her foot.

Heidi took one step, as though she were going to dribble toward the goal. Then, just as suddenly, she stopped again, stepped back, and *fired!*

The shot was low and hard, but it was right at the goalie.

He reached down and . . . *thunk* . . . the ball hit the goalie's hand. At the same time, it slammed into the side of his leg.

But the goalie hadn't been able to get both hands on the ball.

It had glanced off his leg and into the net.

Goal!

It took Nate a second to realize that the ball had gotten into the goal. Then he jumped in the air and shouted.

He had jumped off his good foot, and he tried to come down on it, too. But he got a little off balance, and he ended up tumbling to the ground.

But no one was paying any attention to Nate. The Pride players were all mobbing Heidi.

"See, Jared," Nate yelled as he used a crutch to get up. "We're okay. We'll still beat these guys."

Jared grinned, and he yelled, "Okay. I'll try to stop them now." He looked a little better.

Once the excitement had died down, Nate told Jared, "Their goalie could have had that. But it was a hard shot, and he didn't turn into the ball enough. It's easy to do, Jared. Remember—everyone makes mistakes."

"Okay," Jared said, and he seemed to accept that. He looked ready to play some tough defense and watch his team make a comeback.

Nate was hoping for the best.

But the Bandits weren't about to give up. They were still leading, and Nate had never seen them play so hard.

The next time Oshima got the ball he seemed to make up his mind he was going to score if it killed him.

And Sterling looked just as sure that he wasn't going to let himself get beat again.

He hung right on Oshima and forced him wide. And then, when Oshima tried to cut the ball and reverse his direction, Sterling made a sliding tackle and knocked the ball away.

But Sterling couldn't get up fast enough to run the ball down, and it bounced across the touchline.

The Bandits had a throw-in. Nate watched Oshima walk toward the center of the field and then suddenly burst back toward the touchline.

But Sterling was still playing Oshima tough, and the wing couldn't get the ball to him.

A midfielder took the throw, controlled it off his chest, and then faced Clayton.

Nate had a feeling the Pride players were starting to take over on defense. Any second something good was going to happen on attack.

That must have been what Clayton was thinking, too. He stayed back for a few seconds, as though he were going to leave the midfielder some room. Then he suddenly jumped forward and made his tackle.

The ball bounced off the midfielder's shins and then off Clayton's. But neither could get control of the ball, and it rolled off to Clayton's right.

Oshima and Sterling had seen what was coming, and they both dashed for the ball. Oshima had the angle, however, and he got there first. He didn't try to control the ball, but he knocked it upfield.

That's when Jacob saw it coming and stepped up to take it on a short bounce. But he misjudged the ball. It hit just in front of him and then bounced higher than he expected. It glanced off his foot and bounced toward the goal area.

Jared should have seen what was coming and charged the ball. "Go after it!" Nate screamed.

If Jared had made a quick move, he could have dived on the ball and kept it away from the Bandits.

But the moment's hesitation was too much. When Jared did finally make his move, he suddenly realized that the right wing, Cheri Beesley, was going to get there first.

He threw on the brakes, but he was caught halfway between the ball and the goal.

"No, no!" Nate screamed. "Charge her."

But it was too late. She *smashed* the ball right past Jared's legs before he could move.

Now the score was 3 to 1, and that wasn't the worst part. This goal really *was* Jared's fault, and there wasn't much that Nate could tell him.

"That's all right," Nate said. "We've got a

long way to go. We're still going to win this match."

But the life had gone out of Nate's voice. And the hope was gone from Jared's eyes. He was right back to where he had been earlier.

The Bandits, meanwhile, were going wild. They could smell a victory, and they were already starting to celebrate.

The Pride players knew what it was like to feel that way. Heidi yelled, "We're not finished! Let's just play the way we can." But even *she* didn't sound very sure of herself.

Just when Nate thought things couldn't get any worse, he found out he was wrong.

This time the mistake was Brian's, but the result was the same.

Just a minute or so after the last goal, Brian took a pass from Adam Snarr. He stuck his foot out to stop the ball, but he looked away to see where his teammates were.

The ball took a funny bounce and hopped over his foot.

It rolled right to Oshima. Sterling had just

turned to start upfield on attack, and he was out of position to play defense.

Oshima drove for the goal.

Brian hurried over to pick him up.

Oshima and Brian were one-on-one—except for Jared in the goal. That should have been enough. But Brian tried to go after the ball, and he hit Oshima's shoulder and knocked him down.

The whistle sounded immediately.

Penalty kick.

Jared made a gallant effort, but Oshima was too much to handle—for anyone.

Oshima looked to the left and kicked to the right. Jared took the fake to the left and was left lying on the ground as the ball sailed behind him.

Now the score was 4 to 1, and even Nate was beginning to give up.

Not just on the game. But on the whole season.

Nate found himself thinking that it might be better to forget about playing anymore this season. He could let his ankle heal completely and start thinking about spring soccer.

Something inside him said, "I won't feel responsible if I don't play anymore."

But he didn't like thinking that way.

When halftime came, he used his crutches to get over to the team. He told the players, "Come on, you guys, you've got to give it *everything* in the second half."

Some of the players said, "Yeah!"

And Heidi yelled, "Don't worry. We're going to do it." Then she looked over at Jared and said, "Don't give up. Hang in there, and we'll get those goals back. We're better than the Bandits."

She seemed to mean it, too. But Nate wasn't sure that anyone believed her.

Especially Jared. He looked as though he wanted to cry.

★ 6 ★

Time to Play

Coach Toscano let the players get a drink of water. Then he had them sit down in front of him. He had that same happy look on his face as always.

Nate wondered how he could control himself that way.

"Okay, players, you played some good soccer," he told the kids.

The players didn't look as though they had played good soccer. Most of them had their heads down. And Brian said, "We messed up too many times."

"That's right. You did," the coach said. "But that happens."

Nate thought it was time for the coach to

give a speech. He needed to tell the players that if they didn't win today, they were finished.

Or he needed to tell them to go out there and win one for poor old Nate, with the sprained ankle.

Something.

But the coach said, "You played well enough to be ahead by three goals, instead of behind. If you play that hard again, maybe we can still win it. Let's try, okay?"

It was hardly a rousing speech. But something about it seemed right to Nate. The kids had played hard. They didn't need to be chewed out. They had just made a few mistakes. Harping about that would probably only make things worse.

Nate looked around at the players. They did seem to look a little more hopeful.

Heidi got up and said, "Let's get after them hard, right from the beginning. Their fullbacks are getting tired. Let's outrun them and wear them down."

More of the kids got up. Billy, as usual, had something to say, even though he hadn't yet been in the game. "Hey, when we play *hot,* no one can play with us. We can catch up."

The feeling seemed to be spreading around the team. But Nate was watching Jared, who got up and walked toward the coach.

Nate hopped on one foot a little closer, not bothering to use his crutches.

"Coach," Nate heard Jared say, "I'm still not ready to play goalie. Why don't you let Billy play the second half?"

The coach patted Jared on the back. "Hey, Jared, I told you that you would make some mistakes. But you played great most of the time. So hang in there. Our team is going to make you look good in the second half."

Nate said, "Hey, Jared."

Jared turned around.

"The first time I played a match as goalie, I got massacred."

"Really?"

"Yeah. Really. We've just been asking you to be too good too fast."

Jared nodded. Then he looked Nate in the eye. "I'll try to do better in the second half," he said.

"Hey, just do your best."

Meanwhile, the rest of the team seemed to shift into a higher gear.

Bang, right from the start, Heidi went after Wadley, who had the ball, and picked him clean. Then she passed the ball over to Henry, who knocked it over to Lian.

Henry turned on the speed down the touchline, and Lian led him with a high pass. Henry caught up with the ball and controlled it just as the defender was catching up.

Then Henry quickly drove a pass into the goal area.

A Bandit fullback blocked the pass, but when he tried to trap the ball, he let it roll away from him.

And Henry had followed his own pass.

He picked up the ball on the run and blasted a shot at the goal.

The goalie might have stopped it, but a fullback tried to get his foot on the ball and only touched it. The ball changed direction, and the goalie was caught out of position.

Bam! Into the net.

4 to 2.

"That's what we needed!" Nate was

shouting from the sidelines. "Let's get another quick one. Let's get back into this match."

But another goal wasn't as easy to come by.

The Pride defense had taken over the game. Jared didn't have to do anything. The Bandits weren't getting off any shots. But the Pride couldn't get another ball into the net even though they kept getting decent shots, again and again.

Then the Pride got a break. A pushing call against the Bandits set up a direct free kick.

The Bandits set up their wall, and Clayton took the shot against them. He slammed the ball off the legs of one of the defenders, and the ball rolled across the goal area.

Chris Baca ran for the ball and dove with his foot extended, trying to push a shot toward the net.

But a defender dove at the same time, and it was his foot that got to the ball first. The ball bounced away, and the Bandits seemed to be safe. But that's when Lian darted to the ball and snapped it over to Clayton.

The defenders had expected Lian to take

the shot, and the two fullbacks broke toward him at the same time. Clayton had the space he needed. He looped a high shot into the right-hand corner of the goal.

The goalie leaped but couldn't reach it.
4 to 3!

But time had been passing. Six minutes were left in the match, and the Bandits would now be playing all-out defense.

Nate was excited. He could feel the momentum shifting toward the Pride.

A couple of minutes passed with the Bandits packing the defense and clearing the ball as often as they could. They were trying to use up time, and they weren't even trying to score.

Oshima was as quick on defense as he was on attack, and he was working on Clayton, trying to keep him from getting off a shot.

But Oshima proved that he could make mistakes, too.

He stole a pass deep in his own territory. He dribbled away from the goal area and then tried to kick the ball upfield. But he tried to kick too hard, and he slipped. He almost missed the ball, and it rolled only a few feet in front of him.

The Pride had begun to fall back, but Tammy Hill was back-pedaling, still watching Oshima. She saw the bad kick, and she shot over to the ball.

She trapped the ball and yelled, "Attack!" Clayton dashed past Tammy and yelled, "Here! Here!"

She dropped off the pass, and Clayton drove straight for the goal. A couple of fullbacks had played it safe and were in good position. But Clayton faked a pass to his left and then pushed the ball out to his right just as Heidi came flying into the goal area.

She picked up the pass but had no shot, as the other fullback came over to cut her off.

Heidi scooted the ball right back to Clayton. With a defender all over him, he seemed to have no room for a shot or a pass. But he made a quick cut and then unloaded a low driving shot right between the fullback and the goalie.

Both reacted too late, and the ball whipped into the net.

Now the match was *tied!*

Nate yelled to Jared, "We're going to get them now!" And he really believed it.

The team was really up, ready to get one more.

But Jared didn't look that excited, and suddenly Nate realized why. The Bandits had been playing all defense, hoping to hang on to the lead. But now they would have to try to score. And that meant *attack!*

That worried Nate, too.

Time was running out, and if it did, that would mean overtime. And if no one scored during overtime, that would mean a shootout. And that would mean five penalty shots against both goalies.

Now that the Pride had come this far, Nate hated to think what it would do to Jared to have that much pressure on him.

Nate kept yelling encouragement, but he was really nervous. He could see that Oshima had made up his mind to get a goal and save the day.

Oshima was juking and cutting and dribbling. He brought the ball up the field himself. He passed off once, but he got the ball right back and drove upfield again.

Sterling was close on him, giving ground, not taking chances but not giving him a path to the goal either.

The other fullbacks were back, too, and the defense was in a good position.

Oshima had nowhere to go, but he tried to burst past Sterling anyway.

And that's when he got lucky. Sterling broke with him and ran right into Trenton Daynes. Both boys fell to the ground, and Oshima was suddenly on his own.

He knocked the ball a few yards ahead and then charged after it.

This time Jared saw what he had to do. He rushed forward and met Oshima just as he entered the goal area. Jared dove for the ball.

Oshima stabbed at the ball, but he was an instant too late. Jared had it.

And then Jared surprised everyone. He jumped up, took a look, and slammed a solid punt way up the field.

The ball got over most of the defense, and Henry ran it down.

He faked a pass to the center, but then he pushed the ball down the touchline on the left side. Two defenders held him outside, and for a moment they seemed to have him trapped.

But Henry somehow kicked the ball

through them. Then he jumped between the defenders as he darted after the ball. When he reached it, he didn't hesitate. He lobbed a high pass to the goal.

Nate saw the ball arching toward the goal area, and he held his breath. Jacob was running for the ball and so was a Bandit fullback.

Both leaped, and they knocked into each other. Neither got his head on the ball. It bounced off Jacob's shoulder and rolled loose in the goal area.

Clayton, with his quickness and nose for the ball, somehow broke ahead of everyone else. But he was moving away from the goal and had no chance to shoot.

The guy was amazing. He could watch the ball and yet know, somehow, where everyone was. Henry had kept running and was coming to the goal area when Clayton shuffled the ball to him.

Henry rammed it home without missing a step.

The Pride had *done it!*

The game wasn't over—not quite—but in those last couple of minutes Angel Park played like the pride of lions they were named for. No one got near their goal.

Jared stood alone, sometimes nervously glancing over at Nate. He never looked sure of himself until it was all over. When it was, he didn't leap in the air.

He dropped to the ground.

Nate knew the poor kid was exhausted.

★ 7 ★

Getting Back

When all the excitement was over, Nate felt relieved more than anything else. He knew that the Pride had dodged a bullet, and now the team was still alive for the championship.

Nate finally got a chance to talk to Jared alone. "You saved us," Nate told him. "You really came through when you had to."

"I don't know. I got sort of lucky in the second half. I didn't have to stop that many shots."

"Yeah, but you stopped the big one that would have buried us."

Jared smiled when he thought of that, but then he looked down at the ground. "I still don't like playing goalie. It's too much pressure. Do you think you can be back by next week?"

"I don't know, Jared. At least we don't have a match on Monday. And if I can't play on Thursday, you'll have more time to get ready. I can show you some things that would have helped today."

"Just get better, okay?"

That's exactly what Nate hoped he could do. He was pretty sure he could make it back by Thursday.

Heidi and Jacob rode home with Nate and his dad—so they could hang around with Nate for a while.

Nate was actually kind of tired, even though he hadn't played. The worrying was worse than playing, he decided.

Mr. Matheson got some ice from the refrigerator and put it in a plastic bag. Then he put the bag on Nate's ankle and wrapped the whole thing with a towel. Nate sat at the kitchen table with his foot propped up on another chair.

"There are sodas in the refrigerator," Dad said. "And I think there are some cookies around somewhere. I need to run back to the office for just a little while. You kids make yourselves at home."

So Heidi and Jacob found the sodas and the cookies, and they sat down with Nate at the table.

"Oh, man," Jacob said, "I'm so glad we still have a shot at the championship. When we were down by three goals, I thought we might be dead."

"We still have to beat the Springers again. And someone else has to beat them besides us," Nate said.

"I say we don't worry about the other teams," Heidi said. "We just win our matches and see what happens."

"That's right," Jacob said. "Right now we have to worry about the Tornadoes. They're a tougher team than the Bandits."

Nate knew that was true. And that only made him think about the problem he was facing.

Jacob said what Nate was thinking. "Nate, we need you back. Jared did okay today. But the Tornadoes have better shooters. And you know that Roberts is going to mouth off to Jared and get him all upset."

"Maybe you could play on your crutches,"

Heidi said, sounding serious, as usual. "You could just stick those things out and knock down anything they shot at you."

Nate didn't laugh. "I think I can play. I put my weight on my foot a few times today. It's already a *lot* better than it was a couple of days ago."

"I know, Nate," Heidi said. "But when you start turning and twisting and jumping and everything, you could mess it up worse, and then you would be out for the rest of the year."

"If we lose to the Tornadoes, I might as well be out for the rest of the year. The season would be over."

Everyone was silent for a time.

"All I can say," Jacob finally told them, "is that I hope your ankle starts getting better *fast*. By Monday or Tuesday you need to start playing on it a little so you can be ready for Thursday."

That's also what Nate had been thinking.

"This could be a movie," Heidi said. "I can see it all now. *Soccer Hero.*"

"Yeah, right," Nate said.

Heidi was staring off into space, as though

she were seeing the movie. "What a story! The hero limps onto the field. Every step hurts. He plays anyway, and when the match is over, there's nothing but a bloody stump left on the end of his leg. But the great hero smiles through his tears. He's given his heart—and foot—for the team!"

"Yeah, but there has to be some *love* in there somewhere," Jacob said. "Maybe you could be his girl, Heidi. You could run up to him at the end and give him a big old kiss."

"Hey, I'm not kissing any guy walking around on a bloody stump." And then she added, more seriously, "Or any guy dumb enough to play on a bad ankle."

Nate laughed about the movie idea, but he knew Heidi was making a point. Coach Toscano said that he didn't want Nate to play until the ankle was completely healed. But Nate kept telling himself he could play even if it was still hurting some.

He really did like the image of being the guy who plays through the pain and saves the day for his team. Heidi made it seem silly, but Nate had imagined the whole thing just about like that—except for the bloody stump.

Jacob and Heidi hung around for a while after that, but they were getting ready to go when the phone rang. Nate asked Jacob to answer it, so Jacob picked up the phone on the kitchen wall.

Jacob said, "Yeah, he's here." Then he paused and said, "Yeah, it's Jacob." Another long pause followed, and then he said, "You've got to be *kidding! No way!*"

Nate wondered what was going on.

"Are you *sure?*" Jacob asked. "Were you there or did someone just tell you this?"

By then Nate knew what it had to be. The idea was almost too good to hope for.

All the same, Jacob was saying, "Hey, that's great news. Thanks for calling." He hung up the phone and took a long look at Heidi and Nate. He was grinning, and the color behind his freckles was bright pink. "So, can you guess what happened?"

"The Springers lost their match today?"

"You *got it*. We're tied for first. We win the rest of our matches and we're the champs. All we have to worry about is beating the Springers one more time. The other teams are no problem."

Nate let out a wild whoop and pounded his fist on the table. "We're going to do it!" he yelled.

But Heidi didn't seem quite so excited. "You forgot to mention something, Jacob," she said.

"What?"

"The Springers lost to the *Tornadoes*." She let that sink in for a minute, and then she added, "Now we have to beat *them*—and maybe without Nate. Those guys are getting better all the time. When we beat them before it was early in the season."

Now it all hit Nate harder than ever. But it was Jacob who said it. "Nate, you've *got* to be ready to play. Jared won't be able to handle that kind of pressure."

Nate made up his mind right then. Somehow, some way, he was going to play next Thursday.

He kept the ice on for a long time. And before he went to bed that night, he walked around for a while. He wanted to start getting his weight back on his ankle.

It didn't feel bad at all. His dad caught him walking on it and told him to be careful. But Nate thought everyone—except Jacob—had the wrong idea. He needed to start practicing again as soon as possible.

When Saturday morning practice came, Nate spent most of his time working with Jared. But he also walked around on the foot and even did a little juggling.

When the coach warned him to be careful, he said, "Hey, I don't think it's hurt as bad as we thought at first. It's really healing fast. I think I can practice by Monday."

And when Monday came he had the coach tape his ankle really well. Then he did some of the drills with the team. He was being careful—or so he told himself—and didn't push things too fast. But he did all he could stand to do.

The truth was, the ankle hurt a lot. And it really ached when he went to bed that night. But he didn't say that. He told his parents—and his friends—that it felt almost normal.

No matter what, he was going to play on Thursday. He couldn't let that championship slip away now.

When Thursday came his ankle was actually hurting a little more than it had on Monday. He had played on it quite a bit and had once even twisted it just a little. He doubted he could play his very best, but he was going to forget the pain and do what it took to win.

But that's not what he told the doctor. "It doesn't hurt at all now," he told him.

And he went a step further with Coach Toscano. "It's as good as new," he told him. "I can play."

And so the coach sent him out on the field.

Nate didn't like to think about Heidi's stupid movie idea.

Still, he found himself imagining a little fantasy. He would not say a thing about the pain until he had saved the day. And then he would limp off the field and admit that he had suffered. "But I knew I had to do it for the team," he would finally tell everyone.

Naw. It was too corny. He wouldn't do it quite that way. But tucked away in his mind was the idea that he was about to be a hero.

★ 8 ★

Soccer Hero, the Movie

And so the match began, and Nate tried to tell himself that he would play normally. He wouldn't think about the ankle. It would be okay. If it hurt, it hurt, but he wouldn't change the way he played.

He soon found out, however, that when he tried to turn, or make a quick start, the ankle had a mind of its own. It would give way, and he found himself a little slower than usual.

But the way the match was going, that wasn't much of a problem. The Pride players were psyched about being tied for first. They were really going after the Tornadoes.

Roberts had been cocky before the match. He announced that the Tornadoes could beat anyone now. No way would they lose to Angel Park. Maybe he wanted to psych up his own team, but his words seemed to have more of an effect on the Pride.

Three or four minutes into the match, no one had scored, but all the pressure had been on the Tornadoes' goalie. Then the pressure paid off.

Clayton, as usual, made something happen. He took a long shot, which the goalie blocked. But the goalie didn't cradle the ball, and it bounced off his chest. That sent the ball bouncing in front of the goal.

Sterling had helped bring the ball up the field. When the ball bounced loose, he dashed over to it. He whipped a shot right past the Tornadoes' goalie.

So the Pride had the early lead, and Nate was feeling good.

Nate knew that Jared could have handled anything that had come his way so far. On the other hand, Nate could do a lot that Jared couldn't. For one thing, he was better at directing the defense.

But then the match took a strange turn. For a while the two teams battled in the middle of the field, with neither one getting much going.

Then Lian tangled with Roberts, and both of them fell to the ground. Roberts screamed that Lian had knocked him down, and the referee called Lian for charging.

Nate didn't agree, and he thought maybe the young referee had let Roberts make the call.

Roberts had to take his indirect free kick a long way from the goal area.

But Roberts was tricky. He took the kick as quickly as he could. He caught a couple of the Pride players walking down the field. The Tornadoes got a little advantage, and they pushed the ball deep into Pride territory.

Nate got ready, and he yelled to his teammates to cover. For a moment it seemed as if they had gotten back in time. But then "Rocket" Rockwell broke to the goal area and got a good pass from a midfielder.

He had to turn to get off a shot, and he didn't get much on it. But he hit it in a good spot—to Nate's right and near the goalpost.

Nate had time.

He saw the shot all the way.

He stepped to his right and . . .

Suddenly his ankle crumpled under him. Pain shot through his leg.

He felt even more pain as he watched the ball catch the net.

Rockwell jumped in the air and let out a whoop, and Hugh Roberts ran in and grabbed him.

"I *knew* he couldn't move on that bad ankle," Nate heard Roberts say to Rockwell. "Let's get more pressure on him now."

Nate was still lying on his side in the grass. He was in a lot of pain. For a few seconds he thought he would have to leave the field.

But the thought scared him. He had to save the day for his team. He had been telling himself that all week. He was going to play through the pain, no matter what.

When he saw Coach Toscano running toward him, he got up.

Nate put weight on both feet so he wouldn't seem to be favoring the bad ankle. He stood with his hands on his hips and waited. He held his face straight. But the pain was almost more than he could stand.

"Are you all right?" the coach asked as he came closer.

"Sure. I just slipped," Nate said. He took a long breath and tried to control his voice. "I'm fine. I won't let that happen again."

But he was fighting back tears.

"It looked to me as if the ankle gave way on you," Coach Toscano said.

"No. My cleats just slipped or something. My ankle doesn't hurt."

Nate wasn't very comfortable lying this way. But he told himself that it was what he had to do.

For the team.

Coach Toscano looked doubtful. "Nate, you can't ruin that ankle. No game is worth it. And if you can't play your best, you aren't helping the team by being out here."

"I'm fine. Let's play. That's the last goal these guys will score today."

All that was a little closer to the truth than it had seemed a minute or so before. The pain was going away rather quickly, and Nate was now breathing normally. He really did think he could manage.

He was soon right in another way. The

Tornadoes didn't score. The Pride played tough defense and kept Nate from having to make any quick moves.

Nate did fine as long as he could trot ahead and pick up a weak shot. And he avoided long punts.

If the defense could stay this tough, Nate may only have to make a few good saves. He told himself he would just do it, no matter what it took.

The only problem was, he could see that his team was playing more carefully now.

He had the feeling that the players were doubting him a little. They were stacking up on defense and stopping all shooting opportunities. They weren't pressing the attack.

The match settled into a defensive battle, and neither team came close to scoring. When halftime came, the score was still 1 to 1.

Nate walked off the field, and by now he didn't have to try not to limp. The tape held his foot stiff, and that was a little awkward. But he was hot now, and the ankle had seemed to relax.

He would be fine.

But not long after he sat down on the grass, he noticed a change. The longer he had his weight off the foot, the more he could feel the tightness against the tape. And when he decided to get up and walk a little, the pain was worse than before the match.

The ankle was swelling and Nate knew it.

The thought crossed his mind that he should tell the coach. Maybe that would be the smart thing to do—especially if he wanted to be able to play next week.

But if he did that, he would look like a baby. "Oh, Coach, my foot hurts. Take me out." He didn't want to do that.

Jared walked over to him. "You've done a great job, Nate," he said. "I'm glad you're playing."

That made Nate feel better. And it was true, wasn't it? He had only given up one goal.

But he knew something else, and it was Heidi, as usual, who made him think about it. She put her arm on his shoulder. "Nate, I have a feeling this match is going to come down to one big play. Can you make it?"

"Sure."

"You couldn't in the first half."

"I just slipped."

"Maybe you got the coach to believe that. But I was right there. I saw what happened. You didn't slip. Your ankle wouldn't hold."

"Look, Heidi, I may not be at my best," Nate said, "but it's better than putting Jared out there."

"How do you know? He's improved a lot more this week."

"But he forgets. He messes up. One mental mistake could lose the match too, you know."

"Well, *you* have to decide," Heidi said. "But you might be hurting the team, not helping it."

Nate knew that. But he had also heard about the great athletes who pulled their teams through no matter what it took.

And that's what he was going to do.

So Nate walked back onto the field as the second half started. He trotted around on the ankle to loosen it up. But it was killing him, and he was scared of what might happen.

"I'll just do whatever it takes," he told himself. "So what if it hurts?"

But he also kept hearing Heidi's words: "You might be hurting the team, not helping it."

He didn't like to think about that.

★9★

Nate, the Real Hero

The second half started out *hot*. Both teams really wanted to score.

Rockwell was *quick*. He was giving Sterling all he could handle.

And Roberts had all the moves. The Pride doubled him as often as they could. But Rockwell and Roberts together created big problems for the Pride.

Those two managed to work the ball in deep a couple of times. Nate got in a good position, however.

When Rockwell got off a shot, Nate had it all the way. He shuffled over and caught the ball without having to jump or dive.

Nate felt that he was doing what he had to do.

Then Roberts stole a pass in the middle of the field and made a good run toward the goal area. Tammy Hill forced him wide, and he passed off to a wing. But he got the ball back and burst toward the goal. When he saw he was guarded, he suddenly broke off his run and tried a shot.

It was not a hard shot, but it sliced toward the corner of the goal. Nate had to make a quick dive.

He took one step to his left on his good ankle, and he knocked the shot away.

Brian picked up the blocked shot, and he cleared the ball out to Henry. The Pride went on attack.

As the play moved away from Nate, he was satisfied—in a way.

But he also knew two things. First, just as he had shifted his weight to his left foot, he had felt pain shoot through his bad ankle. If he had had to make a quicker move, he might have slipped again.

But that was not the worst. He was fairly sure that if the play had been to the other side, he couldn't have made it.

The Tornadoes might have scored.

He thought about Heidi's words again. Maybe he wasn't being a hero at all.

But Nate still wasn't ready to accept that. He trotted across the goal area. The ankle was holding up. He had held them to one goal, hadn't he?

The Tornadoes' attack was coming at him, and he got ready. This time the Pride players got all over the Tornadoes, and no one could get off a shot.

When Trenton stepped in and got a steal, Nate yelled, "Attack!" He just hoped that this time up the field the Pride could score.

But then Trenton decided to slow up and drop the ball back so that Nate could direct the attack.

Nate took the pass and saw Chris breaking up the touchline. If he could get off a long punt, he could make something happen.

Nate ran forward and got set to kick with his left foot. But as he pushed off the right foot, he felt pain shoot through his ankle again, and his foot gave way a little.

He got off the kick. But he didn't hit it well.

Then Nate's weight came down on the right ankle as he landed. He crumpled to the ground. His first thought was to scramble up so the coach wouldn't notice what had happened. But he knew he couldn't do that.

It wasn't just the pain.

He knew he really couldn't play.

The team didn't need a hero. It needed a victory. It needed a goalie with two feet.

So Nate stayed down. He shouted, "I'm hurt. I'm hurt."

The whistle soon sounded, and the coach ran onto the field. This time Nate didn't pretend. He pulled off his goalie's jersey and handed it over to Jared.

"Okay, Jared, you can do it," he said. "I should have let you play the whole match. Maybe we'd be ahead one to nothing now."

Jared looked nervous. "No. You played great," he said. Then he pulled on the jersey.

Nate hopped off the field, with his arm around the coach for support. He was already yelling, "Okay, Pride. Attack! We've got to score."

But Nate didn't see much change. He could tell that the whole team was still worried. They had traded an injured goalie for a rookie. They didn't have much confidence.

The problem with that was, the match was being played on the Pride defensive end of the field. And sooner or later that was bound to pay off for the Tornadoes.

It wasn't long until Rockwell used his quickness to break away for a pass in front of the goal area. He made a good move to shake Brian, who came up to cover him. And then he danced to his right and blasted a hard shot into the right corner of the goal.

Nate saw the ball heading into the corner of the net. He felt his heart sink as . . .

But Jared dove.

He stretched all the way out, his body almost on the ground. He slammed the ball with his fist and drove it wide of the goal.

There was no way that Nate could have made the play. Not today. And it would have been a great play any day. Jared really was getting better. He had seen where the shot was going, and he had made his move instantly. A week before he would have waited to commit himself and been a split second too late.

Nate was thrilled. A team with two good goalies had a better chance of going all the way. "All right, Jared! *All right!*" he yelled. *"Great* stop!"

Jared gave Nate one quick glance. Then the whole team crowded around him and pounded him on the back.

Jared pushed them away and told them to set up. The Tornadoes had a corner kick coming, and the Pride needed to be ready.

Nate was glad to see Jared taking control of the defense.

The kick came in high across the goal, and Roberts tried to head it in. But Sterling was there, and he leaped higher than Roberts. He headed the ball upfield and Billy trapped it.

Jared bellowed, *"Attack!"* and this time something new happened. The team seemed to be lifted by Jared's save.

The Pride went upfield like a swarm of bees. Clayton passed to Jacob. Jacob got the ball quickly to Henry on the left side.

Henry knocked it right back to Jacob, and Jacob crossed a pass to Clayton.

They were moving, passing quickly, and getting themselves into position. And then

Heidi cut behind Clayton, used him for a screen, and broke down the middle. Clayton stepped to one side and shot her a low pass that slipped past her legs and rolled ahead of her.

She raced hard, caught up, and seemed about to take a shot.

But a fullback was there, ready to block the shot. The goalie was also in a good position.

Heidi stopped. She used the sole of her shoe to drop a pass behind her. Clayton took the ball in stride and cut to the right. The fullback pulled off Heidi to take Clayton. And that's when Clayton flipped the ball back to Heidi.

Wham!

That was it. The goalie had been expecting a shot from Clayton, and he was on the wrong side of the net.

Perfect team work!

The Pride had the lead, 2 to 1.

The only problem was, almost five minutes were still left in the match. Now the Tornadoes would be coming with everything they had.

That meant Jared would be under fire.

But the Angel Park players were ready. They were feeling good now. They were tired, but they turned their defense up a notch anyway.

They kept the Tornadoes from getting another decent shot. Jared handled the ones that did come his way, but he never had to make another really tough save.

And then Tammy Hill picked up a rebound off a shot by Clayton, and she drove a long shot home.

Fullbacks didn't get to shoot that often, and this was her first goal of the year. She jumped all over the place, and the team jumped with her.

The score was 3 to 1, and the Tornadoes knew they were beaten.

They looked lifeless for the rest of the game. The Tornado fans screamed for them to keep trying, but the team's spirit was broken.

When it was all over, Jared attracted a big crowd. The Pride players knew he had made the big play of the match.

Nate was happy, too, but he didn't dare get in the middle of the celebrating players.

For one thing, he could twist his ankle—and by next week he wanted to be *really* ready to play.

So Nate stood all by himself. He felt strange. He couldn't quite forget how much he had wanted to be the hero.

But that's when Coach Toscano walked over to him and put his arm around his shoulder. "You came through," he said.

"What?" Nate turned to look at him. He could hardly believe what he had heard.

"I know how badly you wanted to play. But it took more guts to come off the field than it would have to stay out there. I'm proud of you. You put the team first."

By then Heidi was running over.

"Who would have thunk it?" she said. "Nate, I thought you were going to be the hero by playing your foot down to a stump. And instead, it turns out you won the game by getting your head on straight."

Fair enough.

Nate laughed, and then he gave Heidi a high-five.

Nate felt good about himself.

The players didn't carry him around on

their shoulders. In fact, they gave a lot more attention to Tammy and Jared. But Nate knew he had done the right thing.

And best of all, the team still had a shot at the championship!

League Standings

Kickers	7–2
Pride	7–2
Tornadoes	6–4
Springers	5–4
Bandits	3–7
Racers	4–6
Gila Monsters	1–8

Match 8 Scores:

Pride	5	Kickers	3
Bandits	6	Gila Monsters	2
Tornadoes	2	Racers	1
Springers	bye		

Match 9 Scores:

Pride	5	Bandits	4
Racers	5	Gila Monsters	3
Tornadoes	4	Springers	3
Kickers	bye		

Match 10 Scores:

Tornadoes	7	Bandits	5
Kickers	5	Racers	0
Springers	4	Gila Monsters	3
Pride	bye		

Match 11 Scores:

Pride	3	Tornadoes	1
Bandits	1	Racers	0
Kickers	2	Springers	1
Gila Monsters	bye		

Kickoff

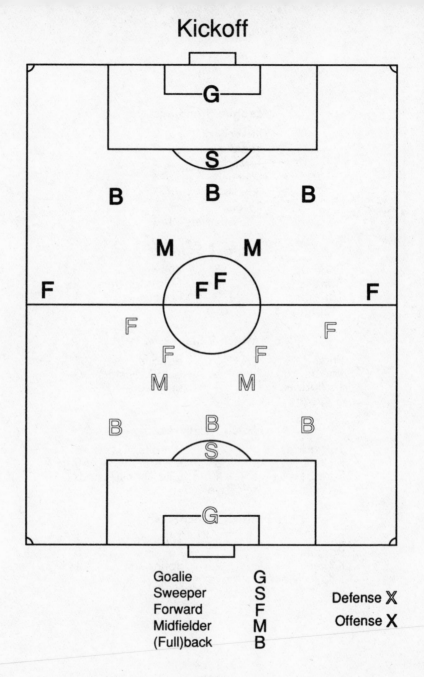

Goalie	G
Sweeper	S
Forward	F
Midfielder	M
(Full)back	B

Defense X
Offense X

Transition Through the Midfield #1

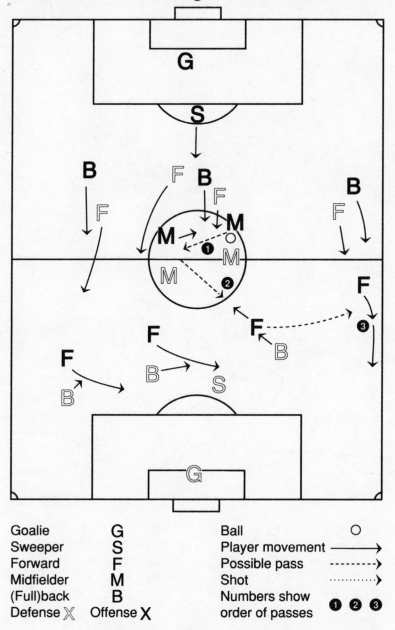

Goalie	G	Ball	O
Sweeper	S	Player movement	⟶
Forward	F	Possible pass	----➤
Midfielder	M	Shot	·····➤
(Full)back	B	Numbers show	❶ ❷ ❸
Defense X	Offense X	order of passes	

99

Indirect Kick #1

Goalie	**G**	Ball	○
Sweeper	**S**	Player movement	⟶
Forward	**F**	Possible pass	⇢
Midfielder	**M**	Shot	⋯⟩
(Full)back	**B**	Defense 𝕏 Offense **X**	

100

Indirect Kick #2

Goalie	G	Ball	O
Sweeper	S	Player movement	⟶
Forward	F	Possible pass	------>
Midfielder	M	Shot	·······>
(Full)back	B	Defense X Offense X	

Throw-in at Midfield

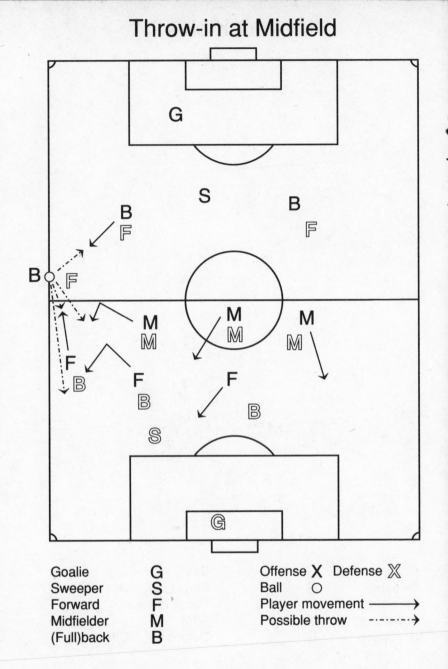

Goalie	G	Offense **X** Defense X̶
Sweeper	S	Ball ◯
Forward	F	Player movement ⟶
Midfielder	M	Possible throw ⤏
(Full)back	B	

Goal Kick

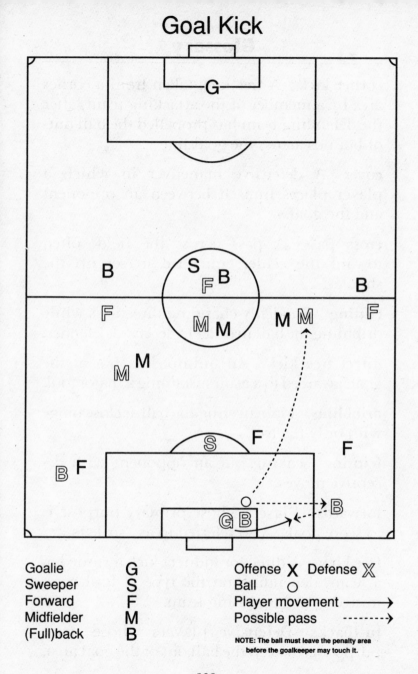

Goalie **G**	Offense **X** Defense **X**
Sweeper **S**	Ball **O**
Forward **F**	Player movement ——→
Midfielder **M**	Possible pass ------→
(Full)back **B**	

**NOTE: The ball must leave the penalty area
before the goalkeeper may touch it.**

Glossary

corner kick A free kick taken from a corner area by a member of the attacking team, after the defending team has propelled the ball out-of-bounds across the goal line.

cover A defensive maneuver in which a player places himself between an opponent and the goal.

cross pass A pass across the field, often toward the center, intended to set up the shooter.

cutting Suddenly changing directions while dribbling the ball in order to deceive a defender.

direct free kick An unimpeded shot at the goal, awarded to a team sustaining a major foul.

dribbling Maneuvering the ball at close range with only the feet.

feinting Faking out an opponent with deceptive moves.

forwards Players whose primary purpose is to score goals. Also referred to as "strikers."

free kick A direct *or* indirect kick awarded to a team, depending on the type of foul committed by the opposing team.

fullbacks Defensive players whose main purpose is to keep the ball out of the goal area.

goalkeeper The ultimate defender against attacks on the goal, and the only player allowed to use his hands.

halfbacks See Midfielders.

heading Propelling the ball with the head, especially the forehead.

indirect free kick A shot at the goal involving at least two players, awarded to a team sustaining a minor foul.

juggling A drill using the thighs, feet, ankles, or head to keep the ball in the air continuously.

kickoff A center place kick which starts the action at the beginning of both the first and second halves or after a goal has been scored.

marking Guarding a particular opponent.

midfielders Players whose main purpose is to get the ball from the defensive players to the forwards. Also called "halfbacks."

penalty kick A direct free kick awarded to a member of the attacking team from a spot 12 yards in front of the goal. All other players must stay outside the penalty area except for the goalie, who must remain stationary until the ball is in play.

punt   A drop kick made by the goalkeeper.

shooting   Making an attempt to score a goal.

strikers   See Forwards.

sweeper   The last player, besides the goalkeeper, to defend the goal against attack.

tackling   Stealing the ball from an opponent by using the feet or a shoulder charge.

total soccer   A system by which players are constantly shifting positions as the team shifts from offense to defense. Also called "positionless soccer."

volley kick   A kick made while the ball is still in the air.

wall   A defensive barrier of players who stand in front of the goal area to aid the goalkeeper against free kicks.

wall pass   This play involves a short pass from one teammate to another, followed by a return pass to the first player as he runs past the defender. Also called the "give-and-go."

wingbacks   Outside fullbacks.

wingers   Outside forwards.